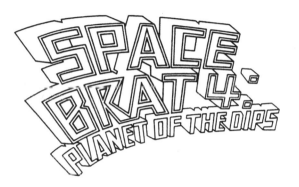

Books by Bruce Coville

The A.I. Gang Trilogy:
Operation Sherlock
Robot Trouble
Forever Begins Tomorrow

Bruce Coville's Alien Adventures:
Aliens Ate My Homework
I Left My Sneakers in Dimension X

Camp Haunted Hills:
How I Survived My Summer Vacation
Some of My Best Friends Are Monsters
The Dinosaur That Followed Me Home

Magic Shop Books:
Jennifer Murdley's Toad
Jeremy Thatcher, Dragon Hatcher
The Monster's Ring

My Teacher Books:
My Teacher Is an Alien
My Teacher Fried My Brains
My Teacher Glows in the Dark
My Teacher Flunked the Planet

Space Brat Books:
Space Brat
Space Brat 2: Blork's Evil Twin
Space Brat 3: The Wrath of Squat
Space Brat 4: Planet of the Dips

The Dragonslayers
Goblins in the Castle
Monster of the Year

Available from MINSTREL Books

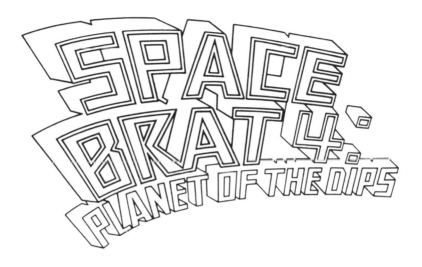

BRUCE COVILLE

Interior illustrations by
Katherine Coville

A MINSTREL® HARDCOVER
PUBLISHED BY POCKET BOOKS

New York   London   Toronto   Sydney   Tokyo   Singapore

For Paula Danziger

A MINSTREL HARDCOVER

 A Minstrel Book published by
POCKET BOOKS, a division of Simon & Schuster Inc.
1230 Avenue of the Americas, New York, NY 10020

Copyright © 1995 by Bruce Coville
Interior illustrations copyright © 1995 by Katherine Coville
Cover illustration copyright © 1995 by Katherine Coville

Library of Congress Cataloging Card Number: 95-069331

ISBN: 0-671-50090-2

First Minstrel Books hardcover printing August 1995

10 9 8 7 6 5 4 3 2 1

A MINSTREL BOOK and colophon are registered trademarks
of Simon & Schuster Inc.

Printed in the U.S.A.

Contents

THE
WHOOPEE
WARP

It was Dr. Pimento's fault, really. Even a mad scientist should know better than to fiddle with a ship's wiring—especially when the ship is about to go into hyperdrive.

But even though Dr. Pimento was brilliant, he didn't have the common sense it takes to sit in a puddle if your butt is on fire.

So the tall, green scientist *did* fiddle with the wires.

This caused Blork's ship to go:

KA-BLAH-BLAH-BLAH-BLAH BLOOMIE!!!
<poop-poop>
Pop!

Blork, Moomie Peevik, and Appus Meko saw stars. Of course, they had already been seeing stars through the ship's viewscreen. But now they saw them *inside* their heads.

The ship shuddered. It juddered. It bounced, jounced, and flounced. It whirled and jiggled. Blork's pet poodnoobie, Lunk, began to whine and drool. (Actually, Lunk drooled all the time. But now he was drooling gallons of poodnoobie slobber, and it was splashing around the cabin.)

Blabber, Moomie Peevik's pet fuzzy-grumper, was so upset he bit his own tail.

"Wowie-Kazowie!" yelled Dr. Pimento. "I didn't expect *this* to happen."

"We're all going to die!" screamed Appus Meko.

"Shut up!" yelled everyone else.

Then no one said anything, because you can't talk while you're being sucked through a Hyperspatial Transdimensional Whoopee Warp. They did *think,* however. And what they thought was:

(a) they were being turned inside out,

(b) it was really strange how the inside of their brains looked purple,

and

(c) feather plumgiddle dimple spek.

(Some things simply don't make sense when you're caught in a Whoopee Warp.)

The strange trip ended as fast as it had begun. They popped out of the Whoopee Warp with a sound something like the love call of a six-thousand-pound fremmis. (The fremmis is the ugliest creature on Blork's home planet, Splat.)

"Dr. Pimento!" cried Blork when he could breathe again. "What have you done?"

"I don't know. But it sure was fun! Want to do it again? Here, this time you hold the wires!"

"I'm not holding anything!" shouted Blork. He felt a tantrum bubbling deep inside him. But captains aren't supposed to have tantrums. So he took three deep breaths. Then he counted until the bubbles were gone.

He had to count to four thousand and sixty-three.

Finally he said, very slowly, "I am not going to hold anything, Dr. Pimento. I just want to know where we are."

"I'll tell you where!" cried Appus Meko. "Lost in space, that's where! We're going to die out here. I just know it."

"Shut up," said everyone.

Moomie Peevik had been fiddling with the computer. "I have a reading, Captain Blork." Her eyes grew wide. "We've gone fourteen *squintillion* miles out of our way!" She punched a few more buttons. "We're close to a planet, but I can't find out anything about it. It's listed as restricted."

"Neat!" said Blork. "I always wanted to explore a restricted planet."

"Are you kidding?" cried Appus Meko. "There could be all kinds of horrible things down there: Huge monsters! Weird diseases! Schools that don't have summer vacation!"

Blork tried to think. He had only been captain for about fifteen minutes, and he wasn't sure what to do. It didn't help when the ship made a sound like a metallic sneeze and lurched sideways.

"Captain, we're losing control!" cried Moomie Peevik.

"We'd better land to make repairs," said Blork.

"We can't land!" screamed Appus Meko. "We'll all die!"

"Would you rather float aimlessly in space for the next several thousand years?" snapped Blork.

"Fine," said Appus Meko. "Have it your way." Then he threw himself against the wall, slid down, and began to sulk.

Blork and Moomie Peevik plotted a course that would bring the ship in for a landing. "I just hope I can control her until we get down," said Moomie Peevik nervously.

Blork was hoping the same thing. He had gotten the ship from his enemy Squat after he defeated him on the Planet of Cranky People. Now he was worried that Squat had secretly done something bad to the ship before they blasted off in it.

When he told his fear to Moomie Peevik, she said, "I doubt it. Letting you bring along Dr. Pimento was probably revenge enough."

Blork glanced at the mad scientist. He was standing next to Lunk, patting the poodnoobie on the head. Both of them were drooling. Dr. Pimento was a genius. Lunk

was as dumb as a rock. Even so, they had a lot in common.

"H-o-o-o-old on!" cried Moomie Peevik suddenly.

The ship swooped close to the planet. It pitched and rocked as it came down, throwing the crew from side to side.

"Whoopee!" yelled Dr. Pimento.

"We're all going to die,' groaned Appus Meko. But he did it quietly, so that no one would yell at him.

They skimmed so close to a mountain that its jagged peaks nearly tore out the bottom of the ship. They plunged into a huge lake, then zoomed into the air again.

Blabber was clinging to Dr. Pimento's leg so tightly it looked as if he had been glued on. Lunk was facing the wall, whining and trying to pretend he didn't exist. Appus Meko had crawled underneath Lunk so that he wouldn't have to see what happened. "Are we dead yet?" he asked in a tiny voice.

At last Moomie Peevik brought them down at the edge of a great forest made of springy-looking red and purple trees.

"Good job!" said Blork. "Let's go take a look around."

"Shouldn't we check to make sure the air is safe to breathe?" asked Dr. Pimento.

"I knew that," said Blork, who had actually forgotten all about it. "I just figured since you're the ship's science officer you would take care of it."

"Right-o!" said Dr. Pimento happily. "As it happens, I have a portable atmosphere tester in my pocket. I invented it myself!"

Taking out a box labeled PIMENTO'S PATENTED SNIFF-O-METER, he asked Moomie Peevik to open the ship's door.

"If I do that it will let our air out," she said. "Won't that be a problem if the planet doesn't have any? Or if its air is poison?"

Dr. Pimento looked surprised. "I never thought of that!"

Blork sighed. "Moomie Peevik, ask the computer if the ship has atmosphere sensors."

Moomie Peevik nodded. A few seconds later she said, "Ship reports air is A-OK, Captain Blork!"

Blork smiled "Then out we go!"

"We're gonna die," muttered Appus Meko. "I know it. I just know it."

"You can stay here," said Blork.

"Are you kidding? If you leave me alone, some horrible monster will probably come along and spray poisonous venom on me and I'll slowly and painfully dissolve into a mushy little puddle."

"Suit yourself," said Blork. He pushed the button that opened the ship's door. Then he led the crew down the ramp.

"Not bad," said Moomie Peevik. "In fact, it's kind of pretty!"

Blork agreed. The air was sweet and clean. A cool breeze blew through the red and purple trees. Nearby flowed a pretty little stream.

Blabber ran in circles, babbling and growling in delight. Lunk began to chase a bouncy little animal.

Appus Meko grabbed Blork's arm. "What's that?"

At first Blork thought Appus Meko meant the boingy noise made by the animal Lunk was chasing. Then he heard it, too. Someone was banging on the inside wall of the ship, shouting "Let me out! LET ME OUT OF HERE!"

"I thought we were the only ones on board," whispered Moomie Peevik. "Who can that be?"

2

THE PLANET OF THE DIPS

Blork stared at the ship nervously. "Do you suppose Squat snuck one of his spider-people on board at the last minute?"

"Let's find out!" cried Dr. Pimento.

"You scientists are such troublemakers!" muttered Appus Meko. "Do you want us all to die?"

Dr. Pimento blinked in surprise. "Of

course not! I want to find out who's making that noise!"

"Let me out!" cried the voice. *"LET ME OUT!"*

Moomie Peevik turned to Blork. "What shall we do, Captain?"

Blork scowled. If he had known being captain would mean he had to make *all* the tough decisions, he might not have taken the job. "I suppose we should let whoever it is out," he said at last.

"Goodie!" cried Dr. Pimento, clapping his hands. "I *love* surprises!"

Blork drew his ray gun. The others followed him back into the ship. They couldn't figure out where the voice was coming from, until Blork noticed Lunk standing by a door, whining and drooling. "That's probably the spot," he said. Tiptoeing over to the door, he pulled it open as quietly as he could. Be-

hind the door stood a very short, very round person. He had on tight pants, a polka-dot shirt, and a hat with a propeller on the top.

"What took you so long?" he cried. Then he flicked the propeller with his forefinger. It began to whirl, and he floated into the air.

Hovering in front of Blork, he said, "I could have died waiting for you to let me out!"

The person looked familiar. Finally Blork realized that he had seen him on the Planet of Cranky People. "What are *you* doing on our ship?" he asked.

"Escaping! I couldn't stand that place any longer." He looked around. "Where are we?"

"We don't have the slightest idea," said Dr. Pimento proudly.

"Great," said the little man. "I feel like I'm back where I started." He floated to the ship's main door, looked through it, and gasped in horror. "I *am* back where I started!"

"What are you talking about?" asked Moomie Peevik.

Before the man could answer, they heard a

commotion outside. Blork and the rest of the crew crowded toward the doorway—which pushed the floating stowaway right through.

"Be careful, can't you!" he snapped, bobbing up and down in front of them.

The others ignored him. They were staring at the cause of the uproar. Tumbling and bumbling out of the red and purple forest came a crowd of laughing, shouting, pushing people. Only the pushing didn't matter much, because each of them was wearing a floating hat, so a shove never did anything worse than send someone drifting through the air.

When the crowd saw the ship, a great cheer went up. "I found it!" everyone shouted. "I found the falling star."

Immediately each turned to his or her nearest neighbor and yelled, *"You* didn't find it! *I* found it!"

Blork was relived to hear that the people spoke Standard Galactic. At least the crew would be able to talk to them.

The crowd was still arguing about who, exactly, had found the ship . . . or star, as they called it. It looked as if a huge fight might break out. Then one of the people shot ahead of the rest of them. He wore a yellow shirt with red polka-dots. His blue shorts were held up with suspenders. Raising his hands, he shouted, "We *all* found it!"

"Cool!" yelled the others. "We all found it! Boy, are we smart!"

"That's not what I heard, you bunch of gibbering nitwits!" shouted the stowaway.

The crowd turned toward the ship.

"It's Skippy!" cried the one who had gotten everyone to stop fighting. "Our beloved Skippy has come back!"

"Skippy, Skippy, Skippy!" shouted everyone else. "Welcome home, Skippy!"

"I think I'm gonna puke," said the stowaway.

"Cool," said Appus Meko. "But point it that way, okay?"

The crowd was surging toward the ship. Half of them were shouting, "Skippy! Skippy!" The other half were muttering, "Who the heck is Skippy?"

"I am, you great flock of fluttering fools!"

"Uh-oh," said Dr. Pimento. "I think I just figured out where we are."

"Where?" asked Blork.

"The Planet of the Dips!"

"Nailed it on the first try, you skinny stick," said Skippy.

Moomie Peevik started to giggle. "If this is the Planet of the Dips, does that mean your full name is Skippy the Dip?"

Skippy sighed. "If you must know, my *full* name is Skippy Dippy Ding-Dong Hooten Pooten Hopbong." He paused, then added, "The *Third*. Which should give you some idea of why I left this place!" He clutched his head. "Oh! I can't believe you brought me back here. I spent half my life trying to get away! I'm so mad I could scream!"

He did scream, which caused Blabber to shriek and jump into Moomie Peevik's arms. "You must have felt right at home back on the Planet of Cranky People," she said, glaring at Skippy.

He looked sad. "I didn't fit in there, either! I'm too cranky for this place, not cranky enough for that one. I was hoping you might take me someplace where I *could* fit in. I can't believe that with a whole galaxy to choose from, you morons decided to come here!"

"We didn't *decide* anything," said Blork.

"Yeah," said Dr. Pimento. "We had a . . . a *discovery!*"

"You mean *you* made some boneheaded mistake!" snorted Skippy.

Dr. Pimento frowned. "Well, you could say that . . . if you want to be *cynical.*"

The conversation was cut off by the arrival of the crowd at the ramp of the ship. "Skippy! Skippy!" they chanted. "Welcome home, Skippy!"

"Whoever you are!" added about half of them.

Skippy sighed. "Couldn't we go somewhere else really really fast?"

Blork shook his head. "We're exploring the galaxy and this is our first stop. So we are not going to run away. Besides, the ship is busted. We have to repair it before we can go anywhere."

"And I want to find out why this place is restricted," put in Dr. Pimento.

"Maybe Galactic Headquarters is afraid stupidity is catching," suggested Appus Meko.

"Nah," said Blork, patting Lunk fondly. "Then they would have restricted poodnoobies, too."

Lunk drooled gratefully.

They were standing at the door of the ship. The crowd of Dips was floating in front of them.

"Greetings, and welcome to our happy home!" said the lead Dip. Holding both hands palms out in front of him, he spread his fingers and said, "Live long and be silly!"

"We come in peace!" replied Blork, imitating the gesture. He thought for a second, then added, "Take us to your leader."

Skippy tapped him on the shoulder.

"What do you want?" snapped Blork.

Skippy looked unhappy. "I *am* their leader," he said with a sigh.

3

THE
TOPLESS
TOWER OF
TIMBOOBIA

We call him the Grand High Dip," said the Dip floating at the front of the crowd. "Actually, these days we call him 'Naughty Naughty Grand High Dip.' He shouldn't have run away. Thank you for bringing him home."

"I don't wanna be here!" shouted Skippy. "I don't belong here!"

Blork knew the feeling. For years he had not felt he belonged on Splat, the planet where he was hatched. (And just when he was starting to think maybe he *did* belong there, he had been stolen by Squat.)

"Will you come back to Timboobia with us?" asked the lead Dip. "If you do, we can have a party."

"What's Timboobia?" asked Blork.

"Our city. You'll like it."

Blork glanced at the others, then remembered that *he* was the captain. "All right, we'll come with you." He thought for a moment, then asked, "If Skippy is your leader, who are you?"

"His name is Beezer the Brilliant," said Skippy. "He was my personal adviser."

"Why do you call him 'the Brilliant'?" asked Moomie Peevik.

"Look at his feet."

Appus Meko began to laugh. "He's only wearing one shoe!"

"Now look at the others," said Skippy. "He's the only one who even got *that* far!"

"Years of practice," said Beezer proudly.

"See what I have to live with?" asked Skippy.

Blork and the crew followed the Dips into the red and purple forest. The Dips didn't have any extra flying hats, so the newcomers had to walk. About half the Dips decided to walk along with them. After about ten minutes, half of *those* Dips got tired and had to fly again.

"How far is it to Timboobia?" asked Blork.

"Depends on whether we go fast or slow," said Beezer cheerfully.

"Well, it's the same *distance* no matter how fast you go," said Moomie Peevik.

Beezer blinked in confusion. "You'll like Skippy's home," he said, changing the subject. "It's a grand old palace. But it's in good shape, because we only built it about five years ago. We call it the Topless Tower of Timboobia."

"Do you call it topless because it's so tall?" asked Blork, remembering a poem about the topless towers of something-or-other that his teacher, Modra Ploogsik, liked to recite.

23

Beezer laughed. "What a silly idea! We call it topless because it doesn't have a roof!"

"Why doesn't it have a roof?"

"We forgot to put it on when we built it."

"Well, couldn't you put one on now?" asked Appus Meko.

Beezer gasped in astonishment. "What a great idea! Somebody write that down!" But after a five minute search, it turned out no one in the group had anything to write with.

"It's no problem," said Moomie Peevik. "We'll just remember until we get to where we're going."

The Dips began to murmur among themselves. "Can you really do that?" asked one of them, her voice filled with awe.

The path led out of the forest and into an orchard. Some of the trees were planted in straight lines, but most were scattered around. A few were arranged in circles or triangles or squares, as if whoever had planted them had gotten sidetracked into trying to make designs.

One section of the orchard had a tall fence around it. Signs on the fence said:

"What's behind the fence?" asked Moomie Peevik.

"Shhhhh!" said Beezer. "That's the Funny Farm. It's where they grow the Sacred Skwishifroot. At least, I think it is. Never mind, I forget. Anyway, it's a secret. Come on, it's almost dark. We have to get back to the city."

"What happens if we don't get back before dark?" asked Blork as they crossed an open field.

"We'll be scared!" said Beezer, leading them into another section of forest.

"Of what?" asked Appus Meko nervously.

Beezer laughed. "The dark, of course."

"But are there things *in* the dark to be

afraid of? Like fierce animals, or monsters, or stuff like that?"

Beezer laughed again. "What a silly idea!"

"But if there's nothing in the dark to be afraid of . . ."

"Don't ask," sighed Skippy. "You won't get anywhere."

"What do you mean he won't get anywhere?" cried Beezer indignantly. "We've gotten somewhere. Look, we're home!"

Leaving the forest—which was just as well, because the poor Dips were constantly bumping into trees—they saw a city.

Rising high above the center of the city was a building that could only be the Topless Tower of Timboobia.

The building was fantastically ramshackle, wider in the middle than at the bottom, then thinner again, then widest of all at the top. Dozens of odd things sprouted from its sides: landing pads for Dips; skywalks that stretched into the air without ever connecting to anything; rickety towers that zigzagged back and forth to wobbly points. Dips flew all around it.

The whole thing looked like the first big wind would blow it over.

"What holds it up?" asked Blork in astonishment.

"Luck," growled Skippy.

"Duct tape, mostly," said Beezer. "Also string, thumbtacks, and a lot of glue."

"And bubble gum," added one of the other Dips. "Don't forget the bubble gum!"

"I helped chew!" cried several proudly.

Blork grew nervous as they walked toward the building. He was afraid it would collapse on top of them if anyone sneezed.

"Don't get too close to the door!" shouted Beezer suddenly.

"Why not?" asked Blork.

The words were barely out of his mouth when the door—which was twice as tall as Dr. Pimento—fell forward with a huge crash.

"That's why," said Beezer softly.

They walked over the door into a huge room. On one side of the room Blork saw several baskets that had ropes tied to their handles. The ropes stretched straight up until they disappeared through holes in the ceiling, which was about fifty feet above them.

"Climb in," said Beezer, gesturing to the baskets.

"What are these for?" asked Blork.

"For going up!"

Appus Meko moaned. "We're all gonna—"

"Don't say it!" snapped Blork. He looked at the others, took a deep breath, then climbed into one of the baskets. Dr. Pimento, Moomie Peevik, and Appus Meko each climbed into a basket of their own. Moomie Peevik was holding Blabber, who kept trying to squirm out of her arms.

Blork climbed out of his own basket and helped Lunk get into the biggest basket they could find. It wasn't easy, and three of Lunk's legs hung over the edge.

"Up!" cried Beezer as soon as they were all settled in. At once the baskets started to rise into the air.

The Dips flew along with them, chattering merrily. Naturally, several of them bumped their heads against the ceiling. "Ow! Ow! Ow!" they cried. "Man, I hate it when that happens!"

Blork's basket was slower than the others.

As he watched, Moomie Peevik made it through to the next floor with no problem.

So did Appus Meko, and Dr. Pimento.

Suddenly Blork heard a horrible squealing. Turning, he saw it came from Lunk. He was stuck. His head and shoulders had made it through to the next level, but his big purple butt was still dangling underneath it. He couldn't go up. He couldn't go down. He just dangled there, hanging on for dear life.

4

THE KING OF SILLINESS

Skippy!" cried Blork as his own basket was drawn up through the floor. "Beezer! We have to do something!"

No one answered him. The Dips were already gathered around the hole where Lunk was stuck. But instead of acting worried, they were shouting and gesturing happily.

Blork climbed out of his basket, then pushed his way through the crowd.

"He's here!" cried Beezer, throwing his arms around Blork and hugging him. "He's here at last!"

"What are you talking about?" asked Blork. Wriggling out of Beezer's grasp, he bent to pat Lunk's head, which was sticking through the floor. Lunk's right front paw had made it through, too. The rest of him still dangled on the other side of the hole.

"You'll see, you'll see!" shouted the Dips happily.

"What are they talking about?" asked Moomie Peevik.

"The Lost Lord of Silliness!" said Beezer, pointing at Lunk's head. "It's him! It's him! He looks just like the statue!"

"I don't care if he looks like the Emperor of Idiots," cried Blork. "We have to get him out of that hole!"

"Oh, yes!" said Beezer. "Definitely! Dips to the rescue!"

A crowd of Dips rushed forward and began to tug at Lunk.

It was no use. He was stuck tight.

Finally a little pink Dip about half the

height of Skippy (but equally round) came over and tugged at Beezer's shirt. "Maybe we should use some . . . you know . . . some . . ."

"We can't do that!" cried Beezer in horror. Then he looked at Lunk. "Or maybe we can. He *is* the Lord of Silliness, after all. . . ."

"What are you talking about?" demanded Blork.

"Fetch the Sacred Goo!" cried Beezer.

Several Dips went scurrying away.

"Well, odds are fifty-fifty that *one* of them will find it," said Skippy.

"Find *what?*" bellowed Blork.

"Some strange new chemical, I hope," said Dr. Pimento, rubbing his hands together eagerly.

"Find this!" said the little Dip who had first tugged at Beezer's shirt. She had returned carrying a round bottle filled with something that looked like reddish-purple jam. She ran over to Lunk and smeared it all around the hole where the poodnoobie was stuck, tucking it through the edge.

Lunk kept stretching out all three of his tongues, trying to lick the goo. Finally the little Dip smeared some of the stuff on Lunk's middle tongue, the medium rough one.

Drooling happily, Lunk pulled in his tongues to do a taste test.

"What is that stuff?" asked Blork again.

"Skwishifroot Goo," said Beezer. "We make it ourselves. It's the slipperiest stuff in the universe. At least, we think it is."

Blork suspected that Beezer might be right, because no sooner had the little Dip finished smearing the stuff around the edge of the

hole than the other Dips were able to pull Lunk through.

The poodnoobie collapsed at the edge of the hole, looking extremely relieved. After a moment he began licking the Skwishifroot Goo out of his fur.

"Well done, Gumbo," said Beezer to the little Dip who had suggested using the goo. He tried to pat her on the head, but her propeller was in the way.

"Thank you, sir," said Gumbo happily. "I always wanted to be a hero!"

Blork thought about pointing out that he himself was such a great hero that he had been summoned to Galactic Headquarters to receive a medal. But he decided that that would sound like bragging.

Giving up on trying to pat Gumbo's head, Beezer put his hand on the little Dip's shoulder. "I hereby appoint you official guide. Show our guests to their rooms!"

Gumbo looked puzzled. "They don't have rooms. They just got here."

"Show them to some rooms they can use," said Beezer patiently.

Gumbo's smile of understanding was so big it almost split her face in half. "Oh, okay! Follow me, you guys!"

Scurrying ahead of them, Gumbo stopped in front of the first door she came to. "This looks good," she said. She pulled it open, stepped through . . . and fell out of sight.

Blork ran to the door. Leaning over the edge, he saw Gumbo floating about ten feet down. The ground was much, *much* farther away.

Moomie Peevik joined Blork at the door. "It's a long way down," she said nervously.

"I knew we should do something about those extra doors," muttered Beezer.

Skippy sighed. *"I'll* find us some rooms. I do know my way around here, after all."

"Wait! Wait!" cried Beezer. "I just realized: The Silly One must go to the Sacred Hall of Goofiness. It is written."

"Written, or scribbled?" sneered Skippy.

"Whatever," shrugged Beezer. "What must be, must . . . must . . ."

"Be?" asked Moomie Peevik.

"That's it!" cried Beezer triumphantly.

"Come on," said Skippy. "I'll find us some rooms."

"Yay for Skippy!" cried the other Dips.

"Yeah, right," said Skippy. "Yay for me. Go on, scram. We'll see you at dinner."

Waving cheerfully, the Dips shouted, "Look out below!" then jumped through the holes in the floor. (Except for five or six who flew through the door Gumbo had opened.)

"All right," said Skippy. "Let's take 'the Silly One' to his room. Then I'll find places for the rest of you."

He didn't sound any too happy.

As Skippy led them from floor to floor, Blork was astonished by the size of the Topless Tower of Timboobia. They traveled by ramp, by baskets attached to ropes, and in one case by ropes without baskets.

Finally Skippy stopped in front of a pair of towering doors. Written on them were the words ABANDON ALL COMMON SENSE, YE WHO ENTER HERE.

"Hey, no problem," said Dr. Pimento cheerfully.

Skippy pushed open the door and gestured

to Lunk. "This is your room," he said. "The Sacred Hall of Goofiness."

The others gasped when they saw the huge room. At the far end stood a raised platform covered with beautiful red cloth.

Lunk went bounding into the room. When he jumped onto the platform, it made an incredibly rude noise.

"The Whoopee Cushion of Glory," said Skippy. He motioned to Blork. "You can stay here, if you want. The rest of you come with me."

Blork went into the huge room. The vast door swung shut behind him. He walked to where Lunk was lolling on the platform, causing it to make ever new versions of the rude sound.

"Well, boy," he said. "Life sure is interesting sometimes."

"You can say that again."

Blork jumped back in astonishment. The words seemed to come from the Whoopee Cushion of Glory.

A little door opened in the bottom of the platform. Out stepped an old man. Tufts of white hair sprouted from his ears, and his wrinkled purple face looked like it held all the wisdom of the world.

"Who are you?" cried Blork.

The old man smiled, showing a single tooth in the bottom of his jaw. "My name is Old Bebop Kenoobie."

"What kind of a name is that?" asked Blork.

The old man shrugged. "I used to be a musician. But my name is not important. What I have to tell you is." Before he could say anything else, the doors at the front of the room swung open. "Uh-oh," said the old man. "I'll see you later!"

He slipped back into the platform.

Blork turned to the front of the room. Beezer was floating toward him.

"What do you want?" asked Blork.

Beezer smiled. "I came to tell you that it is official. The House of Dipresentatives has voted that Lunk is indeed the Lost Lord of Silliness."

"What, exactly, does that mean?"

Beezer looked ecstatic. "The prophesies are true! The Lost Lord of Silliness has returned! Dips can be free and happy!"

"Aren't you free and happy now?"

Beezer waved his arms. "What difference does that make?"

Blork shook his head. "Never mind. Lunk likes this room. I'm sure he'll be glad to be your Lord of Silliness until our ship is ready to go."

"Go?"

"You know: Blast off. Scram. Skedaddle out of here."

Beezer laughed so hard he fell on the floor. "What a silly idea! Lunk isn't going any-where! He has to stay here with us forever!"

5

TRIAL BY
SKWISHIFROOT

Blork stared at Beezer in horror. "You're out of your mind!"

Beezer shrugged. "Well, yeah, probably. So what? It doesn't change things. The Lord of Silliness must stay."

The tantrum feeling was bubbling close to the surface. To push it down, Blork kept talking. "Why do you call Lunk the Lord of Silliness?" he asked.

"I thought you might want to know about

that," replied Beezer. "Come with me and I'll show you. I even brought you a hat."

He held out one of the propeller-topped hats. Blork hesitated for a moment, then put it on his head. He was surprised at how snugly it fit.

"Give the propeller a spin," said Beezer.

Blork flicked it with his finger. Immediately it started to whirl.

Beezer gave him a brief flying lesson, then said, "Think of a wonderful thing!"

"Is that supposed to help me fly?" asked Blork.

"No, it's just nice to do once in a while. Now come on, I have something to show you."

Blork looked at Lunk. "Back soon, boy," he said.

Lunk shifted on the Whoopee Cushion of Glory. It made a huge *SPLORTCH!*, which seemed to amuse him.

Seeing that Lunk was content, Blork patted him on the head, then flew off after Beezer.

They went through the huge doors, then out a big open window. Suddenly Blork realized he was about a thousand feet above the ground.

Grabbing his hat with both hands, he muttered desperately, "Please stay on my head. Oh, please, please, *please* stay on my head!"

They drifted down until they were about ten feet above the ground. Then Beezer led him through the city.

It was the dippiest place Blork had ever seen. People were standing around on rooftops, singing silly songs. He saw ten old men having a funny-face contest—and twenty old women having a squirt-gun war.

About a mile outside of town they came to the edge of the ocean. And there, rising from the sand, Blork saw the Sacred Statue of Silliness.

It was enormous. It was made of some sort of greenish metal.

And it looked just like Lunk.

More to the point, it looked *exactly* as Lunk

had looked when he was caught in the floor of the Topless Tower of Timboobia. This was because most of the statue had been buried beneath the sand. All that could be seen of it was its head and right front paw.

"Awesome," whispered Blork, gazing up at the towering image. "Where did it come from?"

Beezer shrugged. "Don't have the slightest idea. But that's the Lost Lord of Silliness. We have been awaiting his return for centuries. Or maybe it's been five weeks. I forget. Anyway, now that he's here, he has to stay."

"No, he doesn't," said Blork.

"Yes, he does," said Beezer. "It's the rule."

"Doesn't!"

"Does!"

"Doesn't!"

"Does!"

"DOESN'T! DOESN'T! DOESN'T! DOESN'T *SQUARED!*" cried Blork.

He stopped and took a deep breath. He had been right at the edge of having a tantrum, which wouldn't do for a captain.

Beezer looked at him in astonishment. "This can only mean one thing," he said seriously.

"What?" asked Blork.

"We must put the question to the test. And

that can only mean one thing, too: a Trial by Skwishifroot. Luckily for you, the Great Skwishifroot Festival is not far away. Next week, I think. Or maybe tomorrow. Unless it was yesterday. Come on, we'd better go check."

"Wait," said Blork. "What's Trial by Skwishifroot?"

Beezer wouldn't answer. He only laughed. And laughed and laughed and laughed.

Moomie Peevik was waiting for Blork when he got back to the Topless Tower of Timboobia. "Where have you been? I was worried about you."

"Save your worrying for tomorrow. That's when I'll really need it."

Then Blork told her everything Beezer had said about the Skwishifroot Battle—which wasn't much.

"What kind of a contest is it?" asked Moomie Peevik. "How do you win . . . or lose?"

"Beezer wouldn't tell me for sure," said Blork as they went through the doors into Lunk's throne room. "I couldn't tell if he was trying to keep it a secret, or if he just couldn't remember."

Lunk was lying on his back, fast asleep. All three tongues were hanging out of his mouth.

Blork looked at him fondly. "I won't leave you here, buddy," he whispered, tucking in the tongues. "I promise."

"Well, we can hope not," said the voice from under the pedestal. The little door opened, and out stepped the strange old man. Looking from side to side, he put a finger to his purple lips and hissed, "Shhhhh! Don't tell anyone I'm here!"

Since there was no one to tell, that didn't seem like much of a problem.

"Are you a Dip?" asked Moomie Peevik.

"Do I look like one? Never mind, don't answer that. I'm not a Dip, I'm a diplomat. Or I would be, if Galactic Headquarters didn't want to pretend this place doesn't exist. Since you can't send a diplomat some-place that doesn't exist, I guess I'm a spy."

"You're here to spy on the Dips?" asked Blork in surprise. He couldn't imagine why anyone would bother.

Old Bebop Kenoobie shook his head. "No. I'm here to spy on *non*-Dips who visit the planet. The place is restricted, after all."

"I'd sure like to know why," said Moomie Peevik.

"Let me tell you a story," said the old man. He climbed up next to Lunk, causing the Whoopee Cushion to make several disgusting noises. Settling down comfortably, he began:

"Five hundred years ago Dimbo the First led an expedition to this planet. Like so many other people who have gone to new worlds, he was seeking a place where he could live in peace, without persecution."

"Why was he being persecuted?" asked Blork.

Old Bebop Kenoobie frowned. "Dimbo was being hassled by the Forces of Snideness. He and his family were happy little people—too happy for the taste of some. They were always being called brainless idiots for thinking that life is sweet and that people should be able to get along with each other.

" 'We're sappy, but happy,' was Dimbo's motto, and when the Great Migration began, he applied for his own planet."

"Why?" asked Blork.

"He wanted a place where he and his family could live without being constantly sneered at by people who thought niceness was a social disease."

"I'm nice," said Moomie Peevik.

"You're young," replied Old Bebop Kenoobie. "Give it a while. Or maybe things are changing. Anyway, once Dimbo and his people got to this planet, they were quite content. Except when outsiders came to visit. Whenever that happened, sooner or later the visitors would start making fun of them for one reason or another. People started to call it Dimbo's Idiotic Planet, or DIP for short."

"So that's where the word Dip came from!" exclaimed Blork.

"You got it, Bucko. Anyway, Dimbo finally applied to Galactic Headquarters for protection. He didn't get it right away. But finally a great professor, who was secretly a bit of a Dip himself, convinced the Big Boss to think of Dips as an endangered species."

Old Bebop Kenoobie jumped down from Lunk's pedestal. "That's how the Planet of the Dips became restricted. Not because Dips are dangerous for visitors, but because visitors are dangerous for the Dips!

"Of course, these days hardly anyone remembers the place. If they do know about it, they think it's a legend, a fairy tale. But every once in a while someone will search it out."

"Like who?" asked Moomie Peevik.

Old Bebop Kenoobie shrugged. "Usually some cereal company that wants to use the Dips in their advertising. Anyway, because I had made a special study of the Dips, the government appointed me Planetary Guardian. I keep track of anyone who lands here, and make sure they don't harm the Dips."

"What do the Dips think about that?" asked Blork.

The old man put his finger to his lips again. "The Dips aren't supposed to know about me. I am forbidden to meddle in their affairs. My job is to protect them from outsiders. Which is too bad, because otherwise, I might be able to help you out."

"What do you mean?" asked Moomie Peevik.

The old man looked nervous. "I've said too much already."

"Say a little more!" demanded Blork.

Old Bebop looked around nervously. "Things aren't always what they seem at first glance," he said. "Sometimes you have to *dig* for the truth."

He turned and tried to scoot back beneath the pedestal.

"Wait!" cried Blork. He grabbed his arm.

The old man put his hands on Blork's shoulders and looked him in the eyes. "Use the farce, Blork," he whispered. *"Use the farce!"*

Then he ducked through the little door and disappeared.

6

THE FRUIT FLIES

Blork, Moomie Peevik, Appus Meko, Dr. Pimento, and Skippy were sitting in the Sacred Hall of Goofiness, waiting for Blork to be summoned to the Skwishifroot Battle.

"You'll probably die," said Appus Meko gloomily.

"Shut up," replied everyone.

"Tell us again how it goes," said Moomie Peevik to Skippy.

Skippy, who was now wearing a striped

shirt, sighed. This was the third time they had made him tell them the details.

"First we'll go to the SkwishiDome. That's where they have the contest. You will be wearing a white sash, Blork."

Skippy paused, as if seeing it inside his head. When he spoke again, his voice was more excited.

"You'll enter the ring. In the center will be thousands and thousands of pounds of Skwishifroot. The ring-a-dingie will sound to signal the start of the contest. You will be on foot. You will have three opponents, each of them flying. The fruit will fly, too. You throw, they throw. You aim at them, they aim at you. If you hit one of them, he's out. If they hit you, you're still in—unless you get goo on your white sash. That's the rule. No goo on the sash. If you can get all of them out in ten minutes without a stain on your white sash, then you are the winner and can have whatever you choose. But if you lose . . ."

"What?" cried Blork. "What? If I lose, *what*?"

"Probably they cut off your head," said Appus Meko.

Skippy shrugged. "If you lose, Lunk has to stay here."

Blork felt a deep terror growing in him. He couldn't lose Lunk; he just couldn't! "I think I'd rather they did cut off my head," he muttered. "I feel like throwing up."

"Throwing up!" cried Dr. Pimento. "What a great idea. I feel an invention coming on!" He ran from the room. When he returned an hour later, he was carrying a contraption made of sticks and string.

"What the heck is that?" asked Skippy.

"A Skwishifroot Flinger," said Dr. Pimento proudly. "For throwing up, so to speak."

He showed Blork how to use it.

"Thanks," said Blork. But he didn't say it very enthusiastically. He didn't think anything could help him now.

Lunk sat beside him, resting his head on Blork's shoulder. It was heavy, but Blork didn't mind.

The next morning an honor guard of Dips arrived to take Blork to the SkwishiDome.

Kazoos played a fanfare as he entered the arena.

Thousands of Dips filled the stands.

Thousands of tons of Skwishifroot were piled all around.

Beezer stood on a stack of boxes.

"Are you ready, Blork?" he called.

Blork took a deep breath. "I'm ready."

The crowd roared.

"Then let the Skwishifroot Battle begin!" cried Beezer. And with that, he picked up a huge Skwishifroot and flung it at Blork.

"Hey!" cried Blork, dodging to the side. "What are you doing?"

The fruit struck the ground behind him. It was so ripe and soft that it exploded, splashing goo in all directions.

"I am part of the Trio of Skwishers!" cried Beezer, grabbing another fruit.

Suddenly little Gumbo went zooming overhead. "And I'm another!" she cried, throwing a Skwishifroot at Blork's head.

"And I'm the third!" yelled a familiar voice.

Blork spun around. "You, too, Skippy?" he cried.

"Sorry!" yelled Skippy, flinging a Skwishi-froot. "It's the rule!"

Now the fruit flew fast and furious. Blork ducked and dived. He jumped and side-stepped. He dodged and twirled. The crowd cheered and shouted. Dips were jumping up and down in the stands crying "Skwishi! Skwishi! Raw! Raw! Raw!"

Blork used Dr. Pimento's little invention. He flung Skwishifroot with all his might. But no matter how hard and how fast he threw it, he couldn't seem to hit the flying Dips.

Skwishifroot was exploding all around him. Its juice seemed to fill the air. But still his sash was white, still he managed to duck the flying fruit.

Smack! A fruit hit him on the head. *Smek!* Another blobbed against his shoulder. *Smuck!* A third went sailing under his arm. But still his sash stayed white.

Blork's green heart was pounding.

Fling, fling, fling, he threw the fruit. *Zip, zap, zop,* the Dips dodged his best shots until suddenly *POW!* he landed a juicy fruit in the center of Skippy's belly. It erupted in a gusher of goo. Skippy was out of the contest!

Now it was easier for Blork. He only had to watch out for two of them. The blatter blatted. Halftime! Only five minutes to go.

And still his sash was white.

The crowd was going wild. Fruit filled the air. Up in the stands the kazoos were getting clogged with goo.

"Bombs away!" yelled Beezer, soaring overhead. He lobbed an armload of fruit at Blork. Blork bounded away. The fruit exploded harmlessly. Goo was everywhere, but not on his sash. With Dr. Pimento's Patented Skwishifroot Flinger, he sent a *very* ripe skwishifroot sailing after Beezer.

Contact! The fruit went flying up Beezer's pantleg. Skwishifroot Goo came flying out the neck of his shirt, coating his face. Beezer was out of the contest.

Now it was just Blork and Gumbo. But Gumbo was faster than a bird, faster than a bee. She was here, she was there, flinging the fruit like a machine gun. Blork ducked and dodged, leaped and jumped, zigged and zagged. He couldn't hit Gumbo, and though Gumbo hit him, she couldn't soil the sash.

Time was nearly up. The countdown began.

"Ten, nine, eight!" shouted the Dips.

Splot! Splat! Sploot! went the Skwishifroot.

"Seven, six, five!"

Gumbo was hovering overhead. She had another armload of fruit.

Blork took aim with his Skwishifroot Flinger. If he could only get Gumbo out, he would win!

"Four!" roared most of the crowd.

Blork prepared to shoot.

"Uh . . . uh . . . Three!" called a few.

Gumbo threw all her fruit . . . and missed!

"Two!" shouted Beezer the Brilliant.

Blork let fly with the Skwishifroot Flinger.

A gasp of horror rose from the crowd. Then a hush fell over the SkwishiDome.

The Skwishifroot Flinger had backfired.

Flying backward, the final fruit had smashed against Blork's belly. And in that moment Blork's sash, his pure white sash, was spattered with Skwishifroot Juice.

With one second to go, he had lost the contest.

*   *   *

For a moment Blork stood without moving.

"Uh-oh," whispered Appus Meko. "Now we're all gonna die."

Then the tantrum erupted out of Blork.

"NOOOOOOO!" he bellowed. "NO! NO! NO! NO! NO!"

He threw himself to the ground. He kicked. He screamed. He called Dr. Pimento seventeen different kinds of idiot.

Thunder split the sky.

Skwishifroot began exploding all by themselves. Gushers of goo erupted all across the arena.

"CHAA-A-A-A-AR-G-E!" cried Moomie Peevik. Rushing out of the stands to join Blork, she began flinging Skwishifroot in all directions.

Dr. Pimento went running out to join her.

"Oh, man, they're gonna kill us for this!" moaned Appus Meko. He took a deep breath—then rushed in to join the battle.

But the Dips weren't angry, they were astonished. They were also amazed, excited, and delighted.

They began jumping up and down in their seats. Then they started jumping *out* of their seats. They ran into the arena. They threw Skwishifroot in all directions.

The goo ran deep and rich and red.

"Watch me!" cried one of the Dips. He raced forward, threw himself on his belly, and slid all the way to the other side of the arena. Waves of Skwishifroot Goo arced out on either side of him.

"Cool!" cried a thousand tongues, and in an instant a thousand Dips were scooting here and there, sliding, gliding, slipping, skipping, screaming with delight.

"This is the skwishiest party in history!" cried Beezer.

It went on for the entire day, until the Dips were so exhausted they couldn't move.

As darkness fell Beezer stood at the front of the SkwishiDome. "O Mighty Blork!" he cried. "This is the most fun we have ever had. It is our dippiest day ever. We owe you a great boon. Ask and you shall receive. What do you want of us?"

Blork took a deep breath, then bellowed, "I want my poodnoobie back!"

"I meant anything except that!" said Beezer.

Blork began to tremble. But he had already tantrumed once. Another wouldn't do him any good.

Then he remembered the words of Old Bebop Kenoobie. *Use the farce, Blork. Use the farce.*

This had been a farce. And it had given him a second chance. He had to use it.

But how?

How?

7

THE SECRET
OF THE
SAND

Blork thought harder than he ever had before. What else had the old man said?

Things aren't always what they seem at first glance. Sometimes you have to dig for the truth.

Something was nagging at the back of his mind.

The answer was there.

But what was it?

Blork thought about all that had happened to them since they got here.

He thought about their arrival at the Topless Tower of Timboobia.

He thought about his first sight of the Sacred Statue of Silliness, and how much it looked like Lunk when he was stuck halfway through the floor in the topless tower.

And then he had it. Or, at least, he thought he did.

"All right!" he said. "I know what I want."

"What?" cried Beezer. "What is it?"

"What is it?" cried everyone eagerly.

But when Blork told them, a gasp of horror arose from the crowd.

"It can't be done!" cried everyone.

Skippy flew to the front of the arena. "It *will* be done!" he said firmly. "Blork has earned it!"

The next morning a thousand Dips left the city and made their way to the beach.

Each carried a coil of rope across his or her shoulder.

Each had his or her flying hat double-strapped to his or her chin.

Each was ready to do what Blork had asked.

On the beach they tied their ropes to the Sacred Statue of Silliness.

"All right, now pull!" cried Skippy. "Pull, you Dips. *Pull!*"

The Dips flew upward. Their ropes tightened. The statue would not budge.

"Set propellers at maximum!" bellowed Skippy.

The Dips doubled their efforts. They sweated. They groaned. They shook with the strain.

And slowly the statue began to rise from the sands where it had been buried for longer than anyone could remember.

Up, up, up it came. An inch. Two inches. A foot. Three feet.

And as it rose, the truth was seen at last.

Yes, it was a statue of a poodnoobie.

But riding atop it, holding the rope that was tied around its neck, was a Dip.

A Dip that looked just like Gumbo!

At the bottom of the statue was written:

OUR FOUNDER

OUR FOUNDER

"Well, I'll be dipped," said Beezer in amazement. "Lunk isn't the Lord of Silliness after all. Gumbo is!"

"So Lunk is free to go?" asked Blork.

"Of course," said Beezer, who couldn't take his eyes off the statue. "Of course!"

"That can't be Gumbo," whispered Moomie Peevik. "She isn't old enough!"

"Shhhh!" hissed Blork. "It's probably Gumbo's great-great-great-whatever grandfather. But we don't have to tell the Dips that!"

A week later Blork's ship was finally ready to fly again.

"But what do we do now?" asked Appus Meko. "We've gone fourteen squintillion miles out of our way. How will we ever get home?"

Dr. Pimento cleared his throat. "Actually, I've been working on that. Here's what I've figured out. When I crossed those wires and threw us into the Whoopee Warp, the nexus of the warp was at the precise spot where Skippy was standing. That's why we ended up here. *The warp brings you home.*"

"So if we put someone else in that spot, and you mess around with the wires again, we'll end up wherever that person came from?" asked Blork.

"I think so," said Dr. Pimento. He shrugged. "Of course, it's only a theory. . . ."

"Well, let's test it," said Blork. "Now, if we want to get home to Splat, we have to put a Splatoonian in there. I can't do it, of course, since I'm the captain. And Moomie Peevik is the navigator. That leaves . . ."

Appus Meko's eyes bulged in horror. "You've got to be kidding!"

Blork shrugged. "I suppose we could just wander through space for the next hundred years or so."

"Three hundred and forty-two years, to be exact," put in Moomie Peevik.

"Put in Lunk!" cried Appus Meko. "Put in Blabber!"

Dr. Pimento spread his arms. "I'm not sure they would do the trick. Their brains aren't advanced enough."

Appus Meko stood still. He blinked and took a deep breath. Then he threw back his shoulders. He stared at Blork for a moment.

"All right, I'll do it," he said. "You're not the only one who can be a hero!"

The next day the Dips gathered to tell them goodbye. They gave Blork a propeller hat and a white sash.

Skippy came floating up to the door. "Take me with you," he whispered. "Please don't leave me here with these maniacs!"

Blork looked at the others, then remembered that he was the captain. "All right, come on aboard," he said.

Skippy flew in. They closed the doors.

Everyone took his or her place.

"Ready?" asked Blork.

"Ready!" said Appus Meko. He drew himself to his full height, then marched into the closet where Skippy had been hiding when they left the Planet of the Cranky People.

"Ready!" said Moomie Peevik, preparing for blastoff.

"Ready!" said Dr. Pimento happily, grabbing some loose wires.

"Ready!" said Skippy. "And how!"

Lunk drooled.

Blork gave the command.

Moomie Peevik threw the ship into hyper-drive. Dr. Pimento crossed his wires.

"Yow!" cried Appus Meko. "Blabber, what are you doing in here? Ouch! Don't bite!"

"Uh-oh," said Blork

"Cool!" said Dr. Pimento. "Now we can go-o-o-o-o . . ."

With a lurch and a jolt, the ship shuddered into the Whoopee Warp. Where it would spit out the brave little crew, only time would tell.

About the Author and the Illustrator

BRUCE COVILLE was born in Syracuse, New York. As he was a practically perfect child, it is not possible that the character of Blork is in any way based on his own personality. He first became interested in writing when he was in the sixth grade, and decided to write children's books when he read *Winnie-the-Pooh* for the first time at the age of nineteen. (He might have read the book sooner, but he couldn't understand it until then.) Mr. Coville lives in Syracuse with his wife, illustrator Katherine. Coville, and more pets than are really necessary. He has written nearly four dozen books for children, including the bestselling *My Teacher Is an Alien.*

KATHERINE COVILLE is a self-taught artist who is known for her ability to combine finely detailed drawings with a deliciously wacky sense of humor. She is also a toymaker, specializing in creatures hitherto unseen on this planet. Her collaborations with Bruce Coville include *The Monster's Ring, The Foolish Giant, Sarah's Unicorn, Goblins in the Castle, Aliens Ate My Homework,* and the *Space Brat* series.

The Covilles live in a big old brick house, along with a dog named Booger; three cats (Spike, Thunder, and Ozma); and their youngest son, Adam.